To Poppy and Rose

First published in the United States 1991 by
Dial Books for Young Readers
A Division of Penguin Books USA Inc.
375 Hudson Street
New York, New York 10014
Published in Great Britain by Walker Books Ltd
Copyright © 1991 by Bert Kitchen
Printed and bound in Hong Kong
by South China Printing Co. (1988) Ltd.
First Edition
1 3 5 7 9 10 8 6 4 2

Library of Congress Cataloging in Publication Data
Kitchen, Bert.
Pig in a barrow / Bert Kitchen.
p. cm.
Summary: Rhyming verses and illustrations
depict various farm animals.
ISBN 0-8037-0943-9
[1. Domestic animals—Fiction. 2. Stories in rhyme.]
I. Title.
PZ8.3.K65625Pi 1991
[E]—dc20 90-43413 CIP AC

BERT KITCHEN

PIG
IN A BARROW

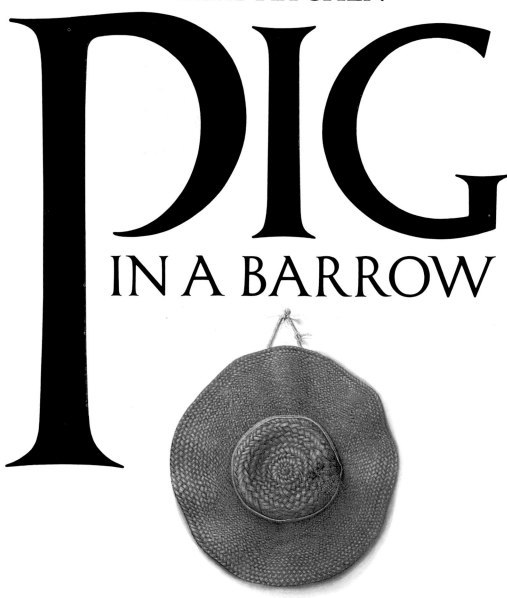

Dial Books for Young Readers New York

Puppy crouching on the scales;
The hand swings past the eight.
Now let's see if this little dog
Has problems with his weight!

The hen in a bucket

Watches her chick,

Who's learning to balance—

A difficult trick.

The bluetit in the birdhouse

Pokes out her little head.

She chirrups to her parents

It's time that she was fed.

This happy pig in a barrow

Has all that a piggy could wish:

Plenty of turnips around him

As he munches his favorite dish.

Ducklings swimming in a tub,

While Mom looks on with joy.

The young ones cannot quite make out

The bobbing plastic toy.

The tortoise in the cardboard box

Has two roofs overhead—

The shell he carries all year round

And the box where he is fed.

The ferret's in a watering can;

Exploring is his habit.

He's always jumping into holes

When looking for a rabbit.

A robin nesting in a boot?

Unusual but true—

These birds don't always build their nests

In trees, as most birds do.

The caterpillar in the jar

Will spin its white cocoon,

From which a lovely butterfly

Will crawl out very soon.

The cat in the basket

Is trying to hide

From Rosie, her playmate,

Who's sitting outside.

Field mice in a parsley pot

Are having fun today.

In and out the holes they go—

A game they love to play.

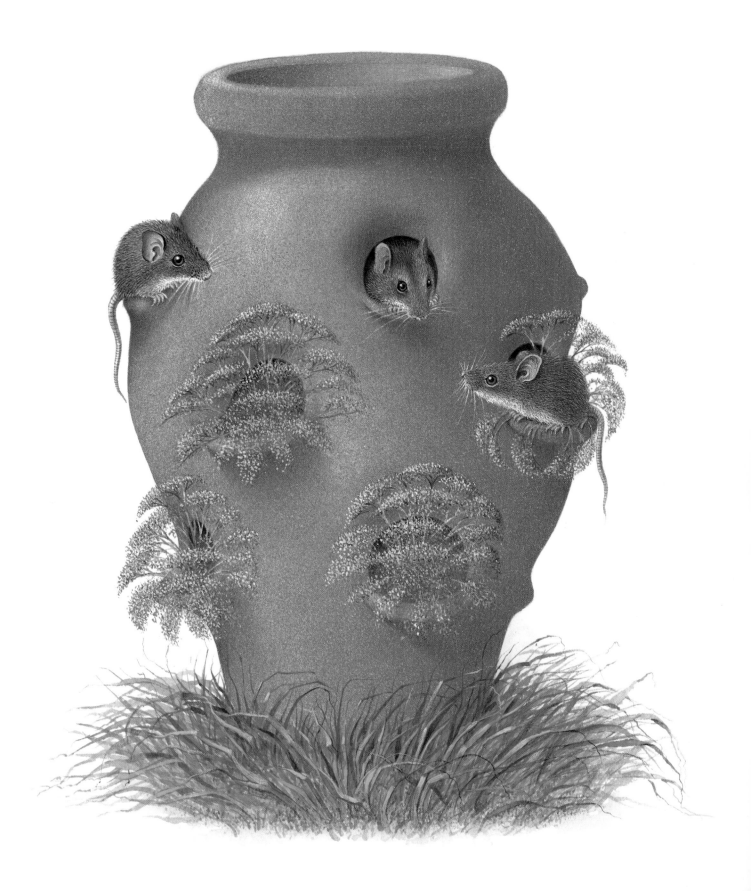

The ladybugs upon the hat

Have found the sprig of heather.

Although not walking hand in hand,

They're keeping close together.